Soar
Your Thoughts
Heavenward

Soar Your Thoughts Heavenward

An Anthology of Christian Poems

Marvet Furze

To order additional copies of this book, contact:
Xlibris
844-714-8691
www.Xlibris.com
Orders@Xlibris.com
839205

CONTENTS

PART 4
Deliverance, Spiritual Warfare

PART 5
Prayer

PART 6
Adoration, Praise, and Thanksgiving

PART 7
Miscellaneous Poems

PART 8
Testimony

PART 9
God Speaks

PART 10
Conclusion

Acknowledgments

I would like to acknowledge the help of God's servants in his work of salvation. The Bible teachers I met at Duluth Seventh-Day Adventist Church did an awesome job of teaching with much clarity, understanding, and zeal. They welcomed new believers even long after baptism. I sat at the feet of Scott Annis and drank spiritual milk after I was awakened from my spiritual slumber and blindness by Pastor Steve Delong. I thank Pastor Cruz for the open, welcoming church he kept.

My hard heart became softened by words of love of God from his servants mentioned above and many more saints of God whom I met. My understanding became clear to put redemption's story in place and Christianity as it is in the Bible.

Thank you, Pastor Wilkie and program coordinators at the Philadelphia Seventh-Day Adventist Church in the Bronx, New York, for the opportunity given to me to share my poetry with the congregation.

Thanks to all my friends who have taken the time to listen to my poetry and critiqued my work. Thanks to my sons who have critiqued my writings.

Thank you, Ramon Beach and Women's Ministry sisters at Allentown Seventh-Day Adventist Church, for listening to my poems online and enjoying them. Thank you, Sis Margaret Ernst, for editing my work. Thanks for the opportunity given to me to encourage others in the continued worship and faithfulness to God.

Thank you, Steve Sergeant, for giving me author's advice. I appreciate all the input of everyone involved from the bottom of my heart. May God bless and keep you as you live and show others the love of Christ in your lives.

Introduction

I wrote this anthology over a period of eleven years on and off. This book is borne from an encouragement and cheer ministry I have on the job plus the special gift I have in writing Christian poetry. I have been writing and reading verses and poems to cheer the sick I care for. I added a Bible verse each time, and both were received well and created joy in their hearts.

The Bible verses used are from the King James version. They encouraged and cheered the sick enough that they awoke, got up, and greeted the day, ready to meet its challenges.

I am writing this book to share with all Christians the gift of encouragement that God has blessed me with. God has been calling me to write (among other things) since my baptism in October 2003. Holy angels were sent to inspire me to write religious poetry. I have put this collection of poems together to cheer and brighten our hope and future in the Lord. This book is written at the right time: the period of COVID-19 lockdown when the entire world is in chaos and fear. The world is experiencing social isolation (a special shut-in) hiding from sickness and death by the coronavirus.

Encouragement is always good; we all could use some at times. At this special time, it is for all Christians—the practicing Christians, the doubtful Christians, the discouraged Christians, the fearful Christians, the spiritually strong and weak, the persecuted, the prospective, and all other peoples of Christian interest—because they will appreciate this literary art form, which is not popular among us. It is good, fun reading material for linguistics scholars.

The aim of this book is to encourage Christians' faith, hope, love, and trust in God in these uncertain times.

Paul, in his first letter, to the Thessalonians, counseled the believers to encourage one another in the Lord and edify each other. All Christians need to look out for one another's welfare at this point.

When earth's problems are humanly unsolvable, then it's time we all look to the highest authority, God, the only all-wise creator, creator of all.

I encourage all Christians to hold steadfast to their faith and continue in prayer, trusting God to deliver on his promise of protection from all evil that will pass over us. Even if he chooses not to deliver, he knows best why.

We can still trust him. God is our refuge to run to. He will not let us down when we need him.

This anthology covers many themes: namely redemption, adoration, praise, thanksgiving, and call to service; God's law of love, grace, and judgment; spiritual warfare, deliverance, and many other aspects. The poems in this book are doctrinal and explain, in a fun way, truths in the Bible that are hard to understand. The poems explain the truth in simple, everyday language. The poems are appealing. They are soothing to the ears but their seriousness appeals to the heart and emotions. Hearing the poems will awaken your thoughts about God and lead you to draw closer to him. We have a lot of time now to get closer to God to know him well. We can give him all the attention that he deserves. He is reaching out to us to save us, so trust him. Our only true hope is in Christ.

Who would think that I would ever write poetry? It's unheard of. No, not me. I was taught to write poetry, but I disliked this writing form, but God selected me to write this book. I told him "no" at first, but then I agreed because God did not give up on asking me. He sent holy angels to my room repeatedly to inspire me with verses and lines of songs and poems. They sang their messages for me.

When I started writing and sharing, the holy angels stopped visiting my room very early in the mornings. Our God is an awesome God. Who can surpass God's power to decide who should do his work?

He gives gifts to the humble and raises up people of low estate, equipping them to do his work. He encourages them to carry out his requests.

It's my privilege and honor to take the opportunity to share with readers in a meaningful, practical way the love of God.

I hope these poems will minister to each reader's heart. God bless your openness and willingness to read about him. I wish a joyful, pleasurable reading experience to all who open the pages of this book.

PART 1

Redemption

The owner of a property is the only true redeemer. God is the only true redeemer of this world, for he made the world and everything in it: he owns it. God will redeem the earth at his appointed time.

Redemption's Plan

Redemption's plan was conceived way back when this world had no
   occupancy,
The Godhead made a
plan very fancy,
They went deep into meditation
about this world's future creation:
Lucifer had no executive pass or entry;

He might have stood guard or sentry.
The meeting was called to order
by none other than the Father.

There was a stipulation
about the people for this world's future creation:
It was: "If man should fall,
who will sacrifice all
for his fall?"
Christ volunteered to
give all for man's fall, even his most precious life:
He volunteered before the earth's foundation began.

God created the earth,
He made Adam and Eve in it,
For Satan this was no cause for mirth,
His covetousness
sparked strife.
He targeted Eve who was less fit.

You see,
Satan lived in heaven where he rebelled and failed to take over
God's authority:
He and his angels were beaten,
They were thrown out of heaven, weakened:
They were made to occupy the vast abyss of the earth.

Satan showed one little fruit to Eve,
convincing her to eat what God forbade,
He knew how to smoothly deceive,
Eve was deceived, and the fruit she ate:
Adam chose to eat, then started to fret:
They knew they did wrong:
They were afraid they had made God upset,
God visited them in hiding,
He gave them a promise.

God's promise of redemption was a plan protected and kept,
Redemption's plan was a
mystery through most of the ages,
Satan misunderstood; he
underrated the plan.
God pronounced His blessings and curses:
He initiated the plan which was instituted.
God redeemed man, marked him forgiven,

A substitute for death was given:
An animal was slain at
first,
Eventually, Christ's life was given.
Adam and Eve peopled the earth,
In this they were very devout.
All their descendants struggled with sin:
To them it was a comfortable thing.
God admonished,
corrected, and cleansed,
impacted, provided,
destroyed, and restored:
He waited patiently and took much time,
His waiting, His seeking to save, was sublime.

His prophets foretold what was so,
Announcing from so long ago,
"Follow the signs, signs of the times:
Jesus will come right on time."

Jesus came to redeem His sinful race,
If you seek for sin in Him you will find no trace;
The plan instituted was partly executed,
So, there's reason for rejoicing:
Jesus came.
It's no shame he gained fame,
For universal
salvation was his aim,

All saints should be
preparing as He has a final appearance.
An appearance to every nation

For the earth's final restored creation:
The plan of redemption
will finally be completed.
God will restore his original, perfect, excellent creation.

Supporting Bible Reference
Genesis 3:15:
"And I will put enmity
between thee and the woman, and between thy seed and her seed,
It shall bruise thy head,
and thou shalt bruise his heel."

The Vision of Jesus's Mission

Who else could Jesus be?
The Son of God and not another,
In the scripture, it's plain to see, even if you seek another.

He was real, on a mission,
To some it was confusion:
His mission they clearly misunderstood, because of false ambition.

He commanded the dumb to talk,
And made the lame men walk,
He cleansed the unclean lepers,
And made the deaf hear.
He opened the blind eyes
to see,
Marvelous light such as His,
The demons cowered at His presence,
Recognizing Him as He truly should be,
He set sin's captives free.
He raised to life the dead,
And spiritual bread He fed,
He filled each empty
head,

And mended their broken hearts,
He lifted the burdens of folks,
He swapped their yokes for His, which was light.

He preached His gospel to the poor.
They learned so much yet yearned for more.
He gave them living water
To quench their thirst for holy wisdom.

He brought for us salvation:
It's made available to every nation.
He died for us a criminal's death,
Fulfilling the plan which was set:
He came back to life, defying death,
Conquering after three
days and nights.

Do we get the vision of Jesus's mission?
It's for everyone who shares in Jesus's passion:
Let's deny ourselves to prepare for the mission,
Put agape love to the utmost test:
Jesus is willing to make up the rest.
Surrender begins the
vision of Jesus's mission,
Submission gives clarity to the vision of His mission,
Expect many persecutions; you can overcome,
Jesus faithfully completed His mission.

Supporting Bible References

1 John 5:5:

"Who is he that overcometh the world, but he that believeth that Jesus is the Son of God?"

Isaiah 35:5, 6:

"Then the eyes of the blind shall be opened, and the ears of the deaf shall be unstopped.

Then shall the lame man leap as an hart, and the tongue of the dumb sing"

The Fulfillment of Jesus's Prophecy: Announcement and His Birth

The angel Gabriel was sent from God to visit the virgin Mary:
A special message was sent to God's selected girl.
"Hail, Mary," he saluted,
"The Lord is with you.
You are a blessed woman,
Highly favored to bring forth God's holy child:
His name shall be Jesus,
Son of the highest:
This lofty baby king shall be born in a humble barn,
He, being the Prince of Peace, shall be one with God."
By reason of love and grace,
Christ came down to save men.
The Holy Spirit
overshadowed Mary and planted the incarnate Christ,
The Holy child to be born would be the Son of God.
Incredible! God Himself to be made accessible,
With God, man would soon interact,
Divinity wrapped in humanity;
Christ came down to

save men,
Born in a stable,
available,
Christ came down to save men,
Who would believe this report?
Only God's devoted servants.

Greatest love story,
Love, incredible, incomprehensible,
Love immeasurable, immemorial,
Yet very true:
The prophecy of Christ's first coming is fulfilled:
He was born to die and live again:
Christ came down to save men.

Supporting Bible reference

Isaiah 7:14:
"Behold, a virgin shall conceive, and bear a son,
and shall call his name
Immanuel."

Christ Came and Will Come Again

Immanuel, God with us,
Christ once lived with men,
In an incredible manner, Christ did come down to men,
To save fallen men at last,
Christ came down to men.
We are blessed and
highly favored,
For Christ will come back for us,
He will collect us as holy trophies,
Christ will come back for us:
To secure us eternally,
Christ will come back for us,
His holy angels accompanying,
Christ will come back for us.
Son of God, wrapped in humanity,
Christ will come back for us.
He shall lead in Holiness;
Christ will come back for us.
He shall lead in Righteousness:
Christ will come back for
us.
With a flaming sword,

Christ will come back for us.
With love unforgettable,
Christ shall reign over us.
With love immeasurable,
Christ shall reign over us.
With love unsurmountable,
Christ shall reign over us.
With love
incomprehensible,
We shall share in Christ's reign.
All saints shall be great in His reign. Amen.

Supporting Bible Reference

Acts1:9–11:
"And when they had spoken these things, while they beheld,
he was taken up; and a
cloud received him out of their sight."

What If

What if Jesus didn't love?
What if Jesus didn't come from above?
What if Jesus made bread when tempted?
What if Jesus hadn't gone to the cross?

Our souls would be counted as dried grass,
To be burned and
eternally lost.
Jesus connected all the way to the cross,
To save all sinful souls that are lost.

He redeemed us for a better place,
A place He prepared for the sin-free human race,
Stay connected, follow only Christ,
He will lead us to His
perfect paradise.

Supporting Bible References

Isaiah 9:19:

"Through the wrath of the Lord of hosts is the land darkened, and the people shall be as the fuel of the fire: no man shall spare his brother."

Luke 19:10

"For the Son of Man is come to seek and to save that which was lost."

The Deception of the Ages

God created the earth:
He made everything in it.
He placed Adam and Eve over it.

Satan became covetous and threw a fit:
He was left out for he just could not fit,
So, he created strife to

ruin it.
He deceived Eve who was less fit.
Adam shared in Eve's wrong choice,
So, they both paid an awful price,
You see, Satan wanted to usurp God's position in heaven,
He conspired with some angels, and they were punished.
They were thrown to this
earth weakened,
They created severe mischief here,
Much more than mere mortal men can bear.
For Adam and Eve, it was
their test.
They both failed, for Adam chose not to resist:
His strong love for Eve took first place, before God,

They fell from grace, and God intervened:

In Eden an animal died to clothe and make them clean.

They lost the light that covered their shame, Exposed, they hid,
   realizing they had reproached God's name.
God triggered the plan He made so long ago:
Redemption's plan
To redeem His people He knew would fall so low.

Supporting Bible References

Genesis 1:1:
"In the beginning God
created the heaven and the earth."

Genesis 3:1–6:
"Now the serpent was more subtil than any beast of the field which
   the Lord God had made, And he said unto the woman, Yea, hath
   God said, Ye shall not eat of the tree of the garden?
And the woman said unto the serpent, We may eat of the fruit of the
   trees of the garden;
But of the fruit of the tree which is in the midst of the garden, God
   hath said, Ye shall not eat of it, neither shall ye touch it, lest ye die.
And the serpent said unto the woman, Ye shall not surely die."

Isaiah 14:12–15:
"How art thou fallen from heaven, O Lucifer, son of the morning!
   how art thou cut down to the ground, which didst weaken the
   Nations!
For thou hast said in thine heart, I will ascend into heaven, I will
   exalt my throne above the stars of God."

PART 2

God's Law of Love, Grace, and Judgment

God is love, and he that dwelleth in love dwelleth in God, and God in him. Herein is our love made perfect that we may have boldness in the day of judgment.

God Loves

God loves; He loves us all:
His grace abounds to man who falls.
Throughout the world, through endless bounds,
His love is pure and truly sound.
You asked me if I'm sure at all?
I'm sure I know He loves
us all.
He waits to catch us when we fall,
And answers when we pray and call.

The love of God flows through us.
It flows through us to those we touch.
We are made with love that God injects,
Lovingly, fearfully, wonderfully made.

Supporting Bible Reference

1 John 4:7, 8:
"Beloved, let us love one another: for love is of God; and everyone
    that loveth is born of God, and knoweth God.
He that loveth not knoweth not God; for God is love."

God's Law in Heaven

God's law in heaven is love, principled love,
More to be desired than fine gold.
God's law is faithful, enduring forever.
The law is His truth embracing his creature's behavior:
In God's presence is perfect law and order,
Without, there is much
disorder.

God joys in peace and harmony.
He locks His heirs in unity.
There should be no contention in God's Holy Nation:
There should be no exception when covetousness is the intention of
    God's creatures.
Punishment is administered with grace.
And mercy is exercised.
All creatures of God's hands are treated with love and fairness.

Lucifer coveted and wished to usurp the throne of the one he was
    made to serve.
God's law was attacked; Lucifer whispered and mocked God's
    Authority.

Lucifer's jealousy aroused his desire to ascend above his maker's
throne.
He conspired with angels and built a case.
False charges were made to secure a conviction.
The charges were, "God, you are unjust: your law, unfair:
Your laws are too many and cannot be kept.
They are burdensome and too much bother.
I have enough reasons to incite my angel brothers."
The court convened; Father God was put on trial.
The charges laid out just could not fit.
Since the charges could not fit, Father God will have to be acquitted.

God's laws must be kept even if Lucifer and some
angels reject them,

God offered mercy, which Lucifer's pride rejected.
God will forever maintain complete law and order:
His loyal subjects will choose to accept.
There should be no confusion in heavenly places:
The price of rejecting God's law and authority is sure separation.

Michael and his angels warred and triumphed. Lucifer and his
angels fought and regretted. They were forced out of heaven with
wounded pride.
They descended to this earth doing well at raising hell on earth:
Their heart was bent on revenge.
They upset God's creation with their own laws and disorder.
Jesus came and defended God's law of love and order.
He lived a sin-free life
vindicating the Father's
Name.
In a little while the earth will be purged and restored.

Only righteous saints will be selected to live in the new earth.
In it will reign everlasting righteousness with perfect love and order.
Amen.

Supporting Bible References

Revelation 12:7–9:
"And there was war in heaven: Michael and his angels fought against
the dragon; and the dragon fought and his angels, And prevailed
not; neither was their place found anymore in heaven. And the
great dragon was cast out, that old serpent, called the Devil, and
Satan, which deceiveth the whole world: He was cast out into the
earth, and his
angels were cast out with him."

Psalm 19:7, 8:
"The law of the Lord is perfect, converting the soul: the testimony of
the Lord is sure, making wise the simple. The statues of the Lord
are right, rejoicing the heart:
The commandment of the Lord is pure, enlightening the eyes."

God's Grace and Judgment

Get ready, get set; Judgment Day is not yet.
The harvest is still on and the reapers are still reaping:
The labor is near ending, so don't quit just yet.
Christ is still pleading and still interceding,
His mercy superseding justice,
His love joined mercy on Calvary's tree.
Christ's blood did flow to cleanse and make sinners free,
To impart grace and mercy to His eternal winners.

In the Father's due time, the judgment will be set,
Honor, awe and reverence will permeate all heavenly places,
Heaven will be jubilant, welcoming all the redeemed,
Who will be waving palm branches in their hands,
The redeemed will create a jubilant scene.

The throne already established is resplendent, glorious and perfectly
    magnificent,
It's more than
mortal eyes have seen,
The Father will be magnificent in His glory,
Seated on His Throne where judgment will proceed;
At His right side will be seated Jesus His Son,

Receiving all due admiration, adoration,

honor, and praise.

Thousand times ten thousand shall minister, Ten thousand times ten
   thousand shall stand,

Dressed in white robes washed in the blood of the Lamb,

Giving worship and praise and thanks and blessings and honor.

The books will be opened; the roll will be

called.

All our secret deeds will be revealed.

The charges will fit:

What will be our plea?

There will be mercy and pardon for you and for me,

The Redeemed will burst forth singing a new song,

A special song of only the Redeemed before the heavenly throng:

They will be given their shining crowns with stars inset,

And hear, "Well done thou

good and faithful servant, enter into the joy of your Lord."

To our Father be blessing, glory, wisdom, and thanksgiving,

And honor and power and might forever.

The unrighteous,

rebellious, pretenders, and scoffers will not be there:

They will wait to perish

in the fire being prepared for Satan and his evil angels.

There will be weeping and gnashing of teeth:

Then will come salvation and strength and the kingdom of our God,

And He shall reign in righteousness for ever

and ever and ever.

Supporting Bible References

2 Peter 3:7:

"But the heavens and the earth, which are now, by the same word are kept in store, reserved unto fire against the day of judgment and perdition of ungodly men."

1 John 4:17:

"Herein is our love made perfect, that we may have boldness in the day of judgment; because as he is, so are we this world."

For God Is Love

We connect to God by love,
We relate to Him in love,
We obey him out of love,
For God is love.

We are created to love.
We should treat ourselves with love.
Our neighbors and enemies need our love too.
God counsels a life of
love;
God exemplifies living love,
For God is love.

God's love is glorious!
He rules and reigns in love.
Esteem God's love highly,
For God is love.

PART 3

Call to Service

Missionary Work: Evangelism

Go ye therefore, and teach all nations, baptizing them in the name of the Father, and of the Son, and of the Holy Ghost: serve the Lord with gladness.

The Lord Has Need of You

Are you tied up with all life's cares?
The Lord has need of you.
Are you messed up with worldly affairs?
The Lord has need of you.

Worldly status matters not.
That can change at the drop of a hat:
Find your purpose, fit in a slot,
Give of yourself for God's worthy cause.
The Lord has need of you.

He needs you at any age you start.
Learn to serve with a willing heart:
He needs you to live the gospel of peace,

To bring glad tidings of good things,
To bring glad tidings of joy:
You are needed to sow the seeds of salvation.
You are needed to water the seeds to harvest.
In time the Holy Spirit will give the increase.

God needs strong heads, strong feet, strong hands.
God needs all ages, all people, to carry out salvation's plan:
He needs young people because they are strong.
Beautiful are the feet of those who fill the gospel needs:
The Lord has need of you,
BUT: you need Him more than you think you do.

Supporting Bible Reference

Isaiah 52:7:

"How beautiful upon the mountains are the feet of him that bringeth good tidings, that publisheth peace; that bringeth good tidings of good, that publisheth salvation; that saith unto Zion, Thy God reigneth!"

My Christian Experience After Baptism

I serve a loving Jesus who is in my heart, I know:
I learn of His requirements through His servants and His words:
I plan to use the gifts I have to gain my starry crown:

I serve different peoples of the world who are zealous for the word.
I share the love of God with them, His goodness and His grace:
I serve the best way I know how to glorify my Lord.
Some care to hear of Jesus's love and His
redemptive plan.
I am working for my Lord and don't care what critics say.
It will make a difference in the life of vile men still alive:
It is a pleasure to my soul to honor and obey.
I bring good cheer to those who are drear and a smile to sad shut-ins.

I recognize the world as a wide evangelistic field.
I will work it when given chances
For it gives me sweet rewards.

Supporting Bible Reference

Romans 10:15:

"And how shall they preach, except they be sent? As it is written, How beautiful are the feet of them that preach the gospel of peace, and bring glad tidings of good

things!"

With All Your Heart

Jesus wants you to seek Him with all your heart
You can find Him,
Seek Him with all your heart and be true.
He already found you,
He's waiting for you to signal to come in,
For His Spirit to live within
To work to make a pure heart,
So, seek Him with all your heart.

Jesus wants you to trust Him with all your heart
You can trust Him:
Trust Him with all your heart and be true.
He's the only one to whom you can give all your heart
And still keep it for yourself in this life,
And keep living till your
end, then live again,
So, trust Him with all your heart.

Jesus wants you to serve Him with all your heart.
He commands it:
Serve Him with all your heart and be true:
He wants it whole, not in part,

So, don't fake it, for He knows it before you start,
So, serve Him with all your heart:

It's His standard; no, not yours:
Do it right by His might,
Serve Him with all your heart.

Supporting Bible References

Jeremiah 29:13:
"And ye shall seek me, and find me, when ye shall search for me with
   all your heart."

Deuteronomy 4:29:
"But if from thence thou shalt seek the Lord thy
God, thou shalt find him, if thou seek him with all thy heart and
   with all thy soul."

PART 4

Deliverance, Spiritual Warfare

Saints of God cannot fight an invisible
spiritual war and win against the devil and his agents in their own
strength.

Call on God to fight for you and the Lord shall fight for you and win.
"Lord, fight against them that fight against me."

The Arms Race

Let wisdom reign:
Technology has gone insane:
To space men race,
Their race is in great haste.

Some nations succeed,
Some nations take heed,
While others go full speed
To get the weapons they need.
A time to kill is their will,
A desire to show evil's secret skill.
Life erased will bring satisfaction,
Forward on! Experience depopulation action.

God doesn't stop this race to kill.
He protects those who obey His will.
Death and destruction will overpass them when
Christ displays his blood—a royal diadem:

Be faithful, be strong; I know we can.
God, forever faithful, secures even the weakest ones.
In the name of Jesus, we have great power:

With God our rock we have great strength:
With God on our side, we can fight and win.
Only in God we are strong:
Only in God we are
secure:
Be faithful to God's holy cause.

Supporting Bible Reference

Psalm 46:1:
"God is our refuge and strength, a very present help in trouble."

Child of God, Be On Guard

Child of God, be on guard:
You are under Satanic watch.
He's selected you to be trashed.
Be aware: his agents are here.
They plan to steal, kill, and destroy.
Satan hatched some evil plans:
He's out to destroy you with his evil hands.
This invisible foe is witty and tricky:
He makes up tricks to put your backs against the pricks:
The trick he picks to destroy you will fit you:
It will trap you without God's intervention.
He will hit your most vulnerable, weakest spot.
Hold on to your faith, for God can deliver you from all Satanic
    attacks.

Satan comes in all forms, all shapes, all colors, all sizes and ages:
Satan's agents are in all nations, all creed, all races, all groups, and
    organizations:
They are dressed in regular suits, some boasting lofty titles.
They are carefully camouflaged and present everywhere:
At nights they are specially dressed to impress all their confederates.
Satan aims to distract all those whom Christ has already delivered:

He wants to put them back in the bondage of sin:
He wants to accuse them again and again, claim them and win.

Satan frequents the highways and holds rallies in the alleys,
He is present in all your circumstances:
Identify him and move him out:
He doesn't belong in our private spaces.
Always take the name of Jesus with you:
It's the main source of comfort for you.
Satan makes you his
greatest enemy.
He wars and carries out his secret, frequent attacks,
But Jesus can always block his attacks:
Be not afraid or alarmed,
He's defeated by Jesus and is subject to His name.
He cowers when he hears the name of Jesus,
He retreats at the sound of His praises
And bolts like lightning from God's true worship service.

Child of God, war only in the name of Jesus.
You can't fight the devils on your own and win.
Child of God, you are followed and being recorded.
Walk carefully, faithfully under Jesus's precious blood:
Don your armor of righteousness, peace, truth, faith, and the word
    of God:
Stand firm; be bold:
God does deliver when He chooses.
Every trial is a lesson: What you learn will make you stronger, wiser.

Stand firm in the Lord and the power of His might:
We wrestle not against flesh and blood:

We wrestle against principalities and powers and rulers in high places,

Rulers of darkness.

We are near the end of earth's sinful ages:

We are on the brink of man-made New World Order.

Protestantism has reached across the abyss and clasped hands with spiritualism:

Satanic worship has gained admiration, and worldwide acceptance.

We are in a serious worldwide worship crisis;

End-time world events create a change in routine living.

Be not deceived or alarmed; be on guard.

Jesus, the captain of the King's Host, stands ready:

He stands ready to war for you with his overpowering right arm.

Supporting Bible Reference

Ephesians 6:12:

"For we wrestle not against flesh and blood, but against principalities, against powers, against the rulers of the darkness of this world, against spiritual wickedness in high places."

I Will Still Praise God

As a root out of dry ground,
Not worthy to be looked upon,
Nothing in my hands I bring,
Faithfully to the cross I cling,
I will praise God.

I've praised God in times of peace:
I've praised God in times of hot warfare:
I'll praise Him in times of my need:
I'll praise Him even if I don't succeed.

I come to Him dependently,
Seeking by faith, Him who is always there,
Who said, "Come in Jesus's name.
"I will grant your petitions made known."
Driven to God to seek His strength,
Abba-Father, fight, for I am weak.
My war has just begun:
It's not mine but yours, so you defend:
I know not why it should begin nor when it's going to end.

Abba, bless me with your presence near me. I have been
encompassed from front to rear:
Evil men and angels intimidate me to drive me to fear.
Shield me, cover me, protect me from powerful foes.
I will continually thank you for seeing me through:
I will still praise you for great strength and peace:
I will still praise you, the rock of my refuge:
I will still praise you, for new thoughts, new hope and a new me.

Lord, Just When I Need You

Lord, just when I need you, you are there:
Waiting to help me, for I am in fear.
Lord, just when I need you, you are my strength:
On you I depend, for you will defend.
Lord, when I need love, you show me you do,
Not forsaking me in trials and woes.
Lord, just when I need you, you are my guide,
Showing the way that in you I can hide.
Lord, just when I need you, you are my shield,
Covering me with your wings where I can abide.
Lord, just when I need you, you are my food.
Feed me, inspire me much, quicken my thoughts:
I need you, my God and my Lord.

PART 5

Prayer

The Christians' means of communication can never be obsolete. God's house is a house of prayer for all peoples.

God still answers prayers.

Prayer Starts a Fire

I've got a burning desire, deep down in my soul:
I've got a burning desire to follow God's holy guide.
It's a fire kindled deep down in my soul:
The Holy Spirit is this fire,
I pray that He stays
within me:
Jesus pours living water to fuel the Spirit's fire.
The just believe and are blessed.
A prayer for you, a prayer for me: for all saints, it's free.

The Holy Ghost transmits our prayers to the Heavenly Father:
Prayer: We can't explain it;
It surely works for us:
Prayer links us to God, our life source.
Prayer keeps the fire, glowing deep within.
Prayer keeps the Holy Spirit working, saving us daily.

Supporting Bible Reference

Romans 8:26, 27:

"For we know not what we should pray for as we ought: but the Spirit itself maketh intercession for us with groanings which cannot be uttered. . . . because he maketh intercession for the saints according to the will of God."

A Christian Believer's Prayer

God of all dominion and power,
All honor and praise are due unto you, Heavenly Father:
We come to you in humility and penitence for our sins:
We come to you in total dependence upon you, Father:
We see our need for you.
Forgive us where we sin against you, Lord, and cleanse us with the
    blood of Jesus.
Judge us with mercy, for we have sinned and come short of your glory,
Bring our surrendered will into harmony with yours, Lord:
Enable us to grow to be more like you, Father,
And fill us with great hearts of love.
Visit us with your grace and favor:
Help us to keep close to you forever:
Thank you, Lord of grace and compassion:
Grant us continual Christian growth to your perfection.
Thank you for your loving kindness every day, gracious God:
We don't deserve you, but your love prevails:
Strengthen us to endure the evil we experience:
Thank you for delivering us from all the evils of each day:
Thank you for saving us in your Holy kingdom.

Keep us loving, pure, good, kind, and true.
Preserve us, comfort us with your Holy Spirit:
Keep us safe by your side eternally, in the name of Jesus I pray.
Amen

Prayer

Prayer links us to God:
He hears: He welcomes,
He answers in wisdom.
He's our All-Wise God.

Prayer releases the power of God on us,
Alerting God to our personal special needs.
Though we can't see the effects, we feel it.
We feel the sensation of God's working power.

Prayer works by faith.
Trust God to give you His reward:
Pray every day, for everything everywhere,
Never forget; you might regret.

Prayer blocks the effects of Satanic power over us.
Baalam's curses against Israel turned into blessings.
Prayer raises God like a man of war:
He will fight for His people's rights.

No apologies from our God of might.
Our warrior God releases terror, brings horror.
All invading evil forces have to retreat, step back:
They can't survive the Almighty God's attack.
Amen

PART 6

Adoration, Praise, and Thanksgiving

"Enter into His gates with thanksgiving, and into his courts with praise: be thankful unto Him and bless his name" (Ps. 100:4–5).

Adoring Heaven's Majesty

Who is like you, O Mighty Father?
Who is like you above the heavens?
Who is like you upon the earth?
For your wisdom and knowledge we are craving.

Just you are in your
words and deeds.
You fill our needs but not our greed:
Your truth is our shield and sword:
Your truth is in your Holy Word.

You hung the clouds in the sky:
You schedule them on time to cry:
You hung the sun and moon in space,
And gave the earth a rugged face.
You tread the lofty tidal waves,
And scale the highest mountain range.
You condescend to man, and save
And love so much we find it strange.

You created your people for frolic and fun,
For your worship and honor and not another's.

You set up presidents: you set up kings:
You inspired David to write and sing:
You put down mighty men of valor,
Shocking them to a deadly pallor.

You hold great men in awe and wonder.
Brilliant minds cannot help but think and ponder,
Searching space way up yonder.
It's no wonder I adore you, Heavenly Father.

Awesome, wonderful, Powerful King,
You show your wrath when repeatedly provoked:
But only for a moment it is evoked:
Who can fight with you and win?
You are our Supreme, Almighty King.

Supporting Bible Reference

Job 38:1–8:
"Then the Lord answered Job out of the whirlwind, and said,
'Who is this that darkeneth counsel by words without knowledge?
Gird up now your loins like a man; for I will demand of thee, and
answer thou me.
Where wast thou when I laid the foundations of the earth?
Declare, if thou hast understanding.
Who had laid the measures thereof, if thou knowest? Or who hath
stretched the line upon it?
Whereupon are the foundations thereof fastened? Or who laid the
cornerstone thereof; When the morning stars sang together, and
all the sons of God shouted for joy?
Or who shut up the sea with doors, when it brake forth, as if it had
issued out of the womb?'"

Admiration of God's Character

Adonai, El Shaddai, Most High God:
We receive and accept knowledge of you:
Almighty God, we praise Your Holy Name.
Jehovah God, we learn of and hang on to all Your promises:
Jehovah Rapha, You heal our bodies of all diseases:
Jehovah Nissi, we love and submit ourselves to You,
Protect us.
Jehovah-Jireh, we benefit from Your providing hands.
Jehovah Tsidkenu, we honor, adore, and trust in You:
Jehovah Gibbor, our mighty God, battles for us and wins,
Jehovah Shalom, we welcome You in our hearts, King of Peace:
Jehovah Sabaoth, we depend on You to secure us,
It's a must.
Jehovah Mekoddishkem, we sharpen our minds with Your words:
Jehovah Makadesh, cover our nakedness; shield us, sanctify us:
Jehovah Shammah, we are witnesses to Your protective care
   everywhere:
God, always faithful, always truthful, always merciful
We give You the highest honor,
We adore You.
God, always there waiting, always helping, always gracious:
We give You the highest praise:

HALLELUJAH!
God always caring, always comforting, always counselling:
We give You all the glory!
God always living, always loving, always watching, we give You our

fullest attention.
Work with us:
Our spiritual battles are Yours,
We give them to You.
Rise up like a man of war and fight for us:
You are our heart's desire:
Our hopes and future are wrapped in You.
God of our thoughts, actions, and desires, guide us, rule over us.
We worship You in the truest sense of human humility:
God of glory, God of honor, praise belongs to you:
God of power and all might, dominion is Yours forever. Amen.

Supporting Bible Reference

Psalm 145:8–10:
"The Lord is gracious, and full of compassion; slow to anger, and of
great mercy. The Lord is good to all: and his tender mercies are
over all his works. All thy works shall praise thee, O Lord, and
thy saints shall bless thee."

A Glance at Our God

In the year King Uzziah died, it made Isaiah sad:
The king is dead, but the King still lives.
Much is being said in Isaiah's vision:
The curtains were pulled back to give Isaiah a glance.
Long live the King!
The most magnificent King is in His glory:
He wears a crown on His head:
His hair is like pure wool:
His garment is whiter than snow.
The train fills His Holy Temple,
The type which angels dare not trample:
He sits on a fiery throne which emits a golden glow.
The smoke rising before Him is slow:
Seraphim stand above His throne, reverencing Him all year round
Praising, singing Hallelujah to the king.
Singing, "Holy, Holy, Holy, Lord God Almighty,
To You belong all honor, all glory and all our praise,
The whole earth is full of Your glory."
Isaiah saw God's purity against his sinfulness.
He was awed when he saw the eternal King.

His countenance is as the sun:
He holds the stars in His hand:
He uses the earth as a footstool:
He stands aloft to survey His domain.
Give adoration, praise, and honor!
He does not die and leave room for another:
He is eternal, pure, and holy:
Long live the King!

Have you seen the king?
Ezekiel, Daniel, and John got a peek:
He is high and lifted up:
With Him all the redeemed shall sup:
Hosts of angels minister always.
His creatures show respect:
They give honor, glory, and praise.
He is worthy of all their praises.
Woe to you when you see the King.
All saints should bow in awe of Him,
Marveling at God's glory which cannot be shared with another.
His glory is the subject of all Saints' songs and stories:
Living with the King never gets saints weary.
Long live the Everlasting King!

Supporting Bible Reference

Isaiah 6:1–4:
"In the year that King Uzziah died I saw also the Lord sitting upon
a throne, high and lifted up, and his train filled the temple.
Above it stood the seraphim: each one had six wings: with twain
he covered his face, and with twain he covered his feet, and with
twain he did fly.

And one cried unto another, and said, Holy, holy, holy, is the Lord
    of hosts: the whole earth is full of his glory.

And the posts of the door moved at the voice of him that cried, and
    the house was filled with smoke."

Praise God, Precious Saints, with Joy

Praise God, precious saints, with joy!
All praises and honor to God Most High:
Praise Adonai, praise El Shaddai:
Lift up God's heart with praises:
Fulfill our purpose here!
He inhabits praise:
Praise our Supreme Authority.

Praise God, precious saints, with joy!
Praise Him, all creatures of His hands:
Praise Him at all your developmental stages:
Praise is due throughout all ages.
Praise God who walked with mankind:
Christ, His Righteous Majesty on high,
To Him belongs honor and praise,
dominion and power forever.

Praise God, precious saints, with joy!
Praise the Creator of heaven and earth:
Praise the Owner of heaven and earth:

Praise Him who fills us with goodness:
Praise God our maintainer and keeper:
Praise God who gives us daily blessings:
Praise the God of unselfishness and fruitfulness.

Praise God, precious saints, with joy!
Praise the Alpha and Omega:
Praise God, the resurrection and the life:
Praise our emotional God who grieves when we sin:
Praise our forgiving God who picks up the fallen:
Praise God, who is full of grace and mercy.

Praise God, precious saints, with joy!
Praise God the Almighty:
Praise Him who teaches our hands to war:
Praise Him who teaches our fingers to fight:
Praise the Captain of the King's Host:
Praise the God of the winning armies:
He wars in righteousness against sin.

Praise God, precious saints, with joy!
Praise the God of perfect beauty:
Praise God, the perfecter of all beautiful saints.
Praise Him for his perfect goodness and love:
Praise God for His perfect grace and forgiveness:
Praise Him for His perfect compassion and mercy:
Praise Him for His perfect patience and longsuffering.
Praise our perfect Sovereign God.

Praise God, precious saints, with joy!
Praise God who has all this world's wealth in His reach:

Praise Him who owns all cattle, fields and all earth's lands:
Praise God who owns all the resources within the lands:
Praise our extremely humble, abundantly wealthy God:
Praise Him who distributes to the righteous as He will:
Praise the omnipresent God: always sharing, always hearing,
always there, always near, always here,
always dear to everyone. Amen.

Supporting Bible Reference

Isaiah 43:21:
"This people have I formed for myself; they shall shew forth my
praise."

Praise God's Sealing Spirit

Word of the Living God renews me, justifies me:
Spirit of the Living God seals me at repentance and baptism.
Blood of Christ cleanses, purifies, and secures me:
Son of God wraps His righteous robe around me.
God prepares and reserves a righteous spot for me:
God, You faithfully fulfill Your promises to me.
Holy Spirit within me, comfort me with Your peace:
Spirit of God, seal me until my day of redemption:
Spirit of God, seal me for my salvation:
Praise God's sealing spirit.
Spirit of the Living God protects and covers me:
Hover over me, filling me with your presence:
Equip me and use me, never to lose me.
Thanks for including me in your redemptive plan:
Inject more love within me, helping me, keeping me:
Spirit of the Living God, seal me for my salvation.
Praise God's sealing spirit.

Supporting Bible Reference

Ephesians 4:30:

"And grieve not the holy Spirit of God, whereby ye are sealed unto the day of redemption."

We Thank You, Lord

Thank you, heavenly Father, for another day,
With bright sunshine and silent clouds that sail away.
Thank you for your weekly Sabbath which we love,
And all your bountiful blessings from above.
We thank you, Lord:

Thank you for your counsel and your care,
And all our friends we can trust without fear.
Thanks for our woes that drive us closer to you:
They test the depth of love we have for you, Lord.
We thank you, Lord.

Thank you for good health from day to day:
And pleasant homes where we stay and pray.
Thank you for all the trials we face:
They prepare us for trying times ahead.
We thank you Lord.

Thank you for the gift of true church friends:
They provide a peaceful atmosphere to stay in.
Thank you for a birthday every year:

You give us time to grow wiser, stronger, and closer to you.
We thank you, Lord.

Thank you for your mercy and your love:
We receive these blessings and many more from above.

Thank you for granting us daily forgiveness:
You give us many chances to clean up our mess.
We thank you, Lord.

Supporting Bible Reference

1 Thessalonians 5:18:
"In everything give thanks: for this is the will of God in Christ Jesus
concerning you."

PART 7

Miscellaneous Poems

We Put on Sin's Chains

We put on sin's chains link by link:
Sin in a blink grows link by link.
Begin today; be lost right away,
Condemned to sorrow if no hopeful tomorrow.

Releasing sin's links can bring great gains.
Zion is where Jesus's righteousness reigns:
There we will have no sin, death, or pain:
We will forever gain
Jesus's righteous liberty.

Together We Can Make
Here a Better Place

Come here, be aware, there is much to hear:
Together we can share
facts about Jesus our Living Savior:
Gather at church, give an ear; there is much to hear

We seem like a rose with
its thorns turned in,
We are beautiful on the outside but hurting within,
Hurting because we inherit terrible sin:
Christ already dealt with our horrible sins.
We pray by faith to overcome this sin nature:
Together we can make here a better place.
With Christ we can make here a better place.

Have we spoiled our todays by yesterday's pranks?
Do our lifestyles put us on a collision course with God?
Are we willing to have the will to do God's will?
Through Christ we can change this course.
We can stay on His spiritual course,
For Christ overcame sin on Calvary's hill.
Do we fear rejection for our faith?

Are we being tossed and bruised with dreaded hate,
Injured, scorned, mocked, and teased
As a passing fancy for those with hateful sin disease?
Together we can overcome; pray without cease:
God on time gives us great relief.
Together we can meet and beat all negatives:
As God's mighty warriors, we can transcend all human barriers.

Jesus can replace hate with love and kindness:
Help us succeed even when we seem to be failing:
We can find safety in an uprising and shelter when it is storming.
Together we can learn and follow the teachings of Christ:
Together we can gain respect in this world.
Righteousness can exalt a people, a nation:
We can rear good families in this place:
We can remove violence from our children's faces.
With Jesus we can live good lives in the worst of all places:
We can do all things through Christ:
We can grow strong in Him:
We can start building God's kingdom here:
Together with Jesus, we can make here a better place.

Supporting Bible Reference

Philippians 4:13:
"I can do all things through Christ which strengtheneth me."

Help Me, Lord

I have wandered far from home:
I am back no more to roam.
Help me, Lord, to live by faith,
And make Jesus Christ my friend.

Thank you, Lord, I see the light.
The devil tries to blind
my sight;
Help me, Lord, to live by faith
And grow stronger with more insight.

For "The just shall live by faith";
I don't have too long to wait,
Help me, Lord, to keep my faith,
Preparing for your soon return.
Direct my life to reflect your ways:
Teach me how to know you better.
Help me, Lord, to live by faith:
Thank you for a converted heart.

Satan gets a huge setback:
Strengthen me for his subtle attacks:

Help me to discern his varied tricks:
Help me, Lord, to live by faith:
Shield me from all of Satan's advances.

Supporting Bible Reference

Isaiah 50:9:
"Behold, the Lord God will help me; who is he that shall condemn me?"

Man's Presumption

Man, you challenge God and turn your back?
Yet God is not on immediate attack.
It is a fact that when God gets ready,
In His own time, He will act.

Man desires to fly in God's face;
From man God will hide His face.
Man is free to make his choice,
Which is his God-given right.

Man titles himself "Ruler" and "King";
With time allowed, man can have his fling with sin.
Christians can always shout, "Hallelujah!" and sing:
Christ is always the King of Kings.
Your time will come; God's vengeance incurred
on stewards whose talents are wasted.

With the earth being God's footstool,
Man should not dare to play the fool.
Man should always take God's part

and stay on His winning narrow path:
Christians can always rejoice and sing,
"Hallelujah!" Christ is always the King of Kings."

Supporting Bible Reference

Exodus 5:2:
"And Pharaoh said, Who is the Lord, that I should obey his voice
to let Israel go? I know not the Lord, neither will I let Israel go."

Just Try Jesus, He's Great!

Brotherman, you love sweet sin:
In this life you
like to do your own thing:
You talk smoothly to charm,
Or intimidatingly with the intent to do harm.
With your character bent,
You need someone godsent,
Just try Jesus; He's sent:
Just try Jesus, for He's great.

He can heal your crooked ways,
Get you walking on spiritual highways,
Change you; give you a total makeover.
A change like this is always better,
Just try Jesus; He's sent:
Just try Jesus, for He's great.

You think you are strong and young.
You have no need for Jesus now:
You crave much more of life's great fun,
But aging takes its toll on fun,

Just try Jesus; He's sent:
Just try Jesus, for He's great.

Jesus loves you, and He's pleading,

He's seeking even those who are not heeding,
He will take you, even if you are messed up.
When you try Jesus; He won't make a fuss:
Just try Jesus; He's sent:
Just try Jesus, for He's great.

Anytime you try him, He will receive you:
He will love you, accept you, and show interest in you:
He will groom you, refine you;
He will fit you for His perfect state.
Just try Jesus; He's sent:
Just try Jesus, for He's great.

Don't wait too long, for time is fleeting,
There's a place prepared for each convert to fit in,
Life lived for Jesus is the best one yet:
Just try Jesus; He's sent:
Just try Jesus, for He's great.

Supporting Bible Reference

John 3:16, 17:
"For God so loved the world, that he gave his only begotten Son, that
whosoever believeth in him should not perish, but have everlasting
life.
For God sent not his Son into the world to condemn the world; but
that the world through him might be saved."

Unfallen People: Adam and Eve

God decided to people the earth.
He took some specks of dust he found
Lying beside him on the ground:
He molded the dust to form a man,
Then breathed into his nose.
Adam screamed when he took his first breath,
He practiced the rest with greater ease,
And God said, "You are Adam, my first handmade.
Now you can get up and praise and sing."
Adam sang, "I am a man, my name is Adam. I am now your favorite
    being."
God proclaimed his work very good:
He felt content to behold the first man he made on earth.
In the image of God created He Adam,
Imparting to him a measure of the divine attributes.
God gave Adam a handsome face:
He made Adam for his fun and pleasure:
Adam was pampered at God's great leisure.
Adam enjoyed the nuts, fruits, and vegetables,
The land and water animals and lush green fields,

He dominated and nurtured all things new.
He noticed each of the animals had a mate,
For Adam his mate came not too late,
God operated and produced for him a perfect mate
A rib was surgically
removed and miraculously became the wife of his life.
To have and to hold, to love and be bold,
For giving and taking while rooming and grooming:
He cherished the wife of his life.
Adam stood full size: absolutely, perfectly tall,
He admired his wife; he was intrigued by her beauty,
They both stood stately in dignity and integrity:
Their muscles rippled; their skins glowed in great health:
They related and served their loving Father in honor and respect.
Ooh! How beautiful they appeared:
They were in all their perfect glory, shining brightly:
They were made in the image of their loving Father.
They should always remember God, their
Designer, Creator, and highest Authority.
God made man, which is true, but Satan hatched many disputed,
    age-old stories.

Supporting Bible References

Genesis 2:7:
"And the Lord God formed man of the dust of the ground, and
    breathed into his nostrils the breath of life; and man became a
    living soul."

Genesis 2:21, 22:

"And the Lord God caused a deep sleep to fall upon Adam, and he
slept: and he took one of his ribs, and closed up the flesh instead
thereof; And the rib, which the Lord had taken from man, made
he a woman, and brought her unto the man."

I Wonder

I wonder at the power of God to clothe himself with burning light:
He doesn't get burned.
I wonder at God's great strength to hold the world in his hands:
He never gets tired.
I wonder at the speed of God who travels faster than the speed of
   light,
Yet he doesn't have a
collision.
I wonder at the size of God's feet that rest upon the earth:
The earth as his footstool is not too big.
I wonder at God's roving eyes seeing everything everywhere here:
They go through and through the whole earth.
I wonder at God's skill and ability to ride upon the wings of the wind:
He keeps it under control.
I wonder at God's order, ordaining the sun, moon, and stars to shine
   their lights:
They all come out in perfect order, on time, always in plain sight.
I wonder at a lofty God being humble, seeking to relate to lowly man:
He pushes the proud afar off.
I wonder at God's alluring love drawing the hearts of all men to Him.
I wonder at God's wisdom to keep some trees and grass green in
   winter's killing cold:

He cares for His creation.
I wonder at God's grace and mercy to keep maintaining ungrateful,
    insulting, provoking men,
Yet God never sinned

Himself.
I wonder at the power of God's stare:
He looks at the hills and they tremble and smoke.
The earth is waxing old as a garment:
Nature as obedient as it used to be, is being worn out:
Men change for the worse as they continually disobey God's laws.
God has perfect love and
compassion, wisdom, knowledge, and understanding.
No wonder God is God, set apart, unique; clothed in majesty and
    mystery.
Amen.

PART 8

Testimony

There is no testimony without a test.

God's Deliverance: A Personal Testimony of Spiritual Warfare

So many people were sent to look at me and took many pictures
of me.
Am I a huge celebrity or important figure of authority?
I think not, just an ordinary person, a regular Christian woman.
They took disadvantage of my spiritual ignorance:
They drew near to me to discomfit me,
But as my custom was, I praised God:
I was always praising God in the mornings and evenings.

The constant stream of people who came to look at me said,
"That is not her, but we will follow.
She is not from here and she can take us to the one we really want
to find."
My best friend ran away in fear:
They centered their negative attention on me.
I became suspicious and fearful, not knowing what would ensue,
I continued to praise God no matter what,
They harassed me, followed me, using intimidatory tactics to
scare me:
I sensed secret meetings planning to destroy me.
Evil forces moved close by to monitor my every movement:

They planned how best to hurt me,

Everywhere I visited or hung out in comfort was a snare for me:

Evil devices have been used against me to paralyze me:

Neighbors robbed my restful sleep or allowed it:

The worst of the evil struck at midnight or after I settled down to rest,

When I was alone, tired, when I became still, the devils forced their will.

But I was always praising God!

They targeted my entire body, seeking to ruin my flesh,

But they caught me praising God.

God gave me comfort in dreams, visions, and human messengers.

I decided I could linger a little longer; I did linger.

Strangers drove fear in me, recognizing me after glancing at their cell phones.

They followed me everywhere I went.

They fussed at me, cursed at me, bumped into me, seeking to stop my movement, my progress,

Horns were honked at me,

Sirens serenaded my walks.

All came up against me with hostility that made no sense to me,

Temporary neighbors moved in, terrorized me and tormented me especially at nights.

Indoors I was electrified, needled, spiked, chemically treated, burned, and much more.

Through all this I was fearfully praising God:

I knew he would see me

through as promised.

God did overrule:

He limited and blocked their evil work:

They were not given their evil desires:
However, they teased me, mocked me, and
tortured me greatly:
I was tortured by Satan and his strong demonic princes:
Tortured, targeted for all kinds of destruction:
Tortured that I should not settle down to complete God's work,
Tortured to destroy my body and mind,
Satan's attempts to destroy me were not honored:
I was cast down but not crushed; trampled on, but not destroyed,
New York darkness took hold of me, engulfing me, surrounding me,
Satan's agents swamped me, trying to make a complete mockery out
    of me,
But God saved me:
For through all this I was fearfully praising God.

They did not understand why I could still function:
They did not understand Christ's blood covenant over my life,
I was afflicted but still standing, always praising God.
I suffered, I pained, but still carried on,
I shared in part of the suffering of Christ.
I hope it is not in vain, as I want to reign with Him someday.
He shielded me from imminent destruction,
He moved me away from imminent danger,
I will always praise my God.

My life suddenly changed course for the worse; lost employment, lost
    my savings, lost good health, lost weight, lost clothing, lost food.
Lethargy and physical illness set in:
The Alpha and Omega already knew that this would be, so he made
    a way out for me.

He provided people to help at every junction of the road of this affliction.

I ran to my own and was mistreated, scorned, scoffed at, looked down on, and mocked even more.

Then God lifted me up in the presence of my enemies.
He brushed me off and put me on my feet to stand:
Today I stand more firmly in God, the source of my strength:
I stand in Christ's righteousness, peace, and faith in his promises:
I stand in prayer, praise, and thanksgiving.
God has enlightened me, strengthened me, fought for me, and delivered me.
God has built me for war, spiritual war:
God has taught my hands to war and fingers to fight:
This spiritual warfare carries on, even though God already won.
God will complete the good work he has started in me:
Completion is near to stump the tricks the devils play,
I will always praise God as long as I have breath;
I will always praise God as long as I have a mouth, a head, a voice.
YAHWEH alone is worthy of all my praises. Amen.

Supporting Bible References

Psalm 34:19:
"Many are the afflictions of the righteous: but the Lord delivereth him out of them all."

Isaiah 32:7:
"The instruments also of the churl are evil: he deviseth wicked devices to destroy the poor with lying words, even when the needy speaketh right."

PART 9

God Speaks

Be Still, for God Is God and God Alone

The King of righteousness and peace is present here with us:
We fight in his might.
His Majesty commands us, "Be still, hold your peace:
Be still, for I am God and God alone, the Holy One:
There's no other being like me: no one else like me.
In all your spiritual warfare, I strengthen you from within:
I comfort, fight, teach, and show you things to come.
In turmoil or tranquility, I am near you:
In sickness or good health, I am there for you:
Hold your peace; be still, knowing your strength is in me.
Be not dismayed or afraid, I won't forsake you:
I will fight all your battles given to me.
Run to me; I am your refuge and security:
Only in me you are safe and secure.
Be patient, stand aside and watch me excel in action.
Be still, hold your peace, for I am God and God alone.

All power comes from the I AM who saves you.
Rejoice in the power of my salvation:
Be confident in me when mountains rise above you:

Depend on me when evil faces are set before you.

Consult with me when an evil atmosphere surrounds you:

I will dispatch holy warriors who excel in strength to rescue you:

There are more with us than with the evil legions.

No weapons formed against you can prosper.

When I bless you, no one can block it;

I will turn their curses into your blessings,

Make negatives into positives:

I have almighty power to completely deliver you:

Be still, hold your peace, for I am God and God alone.

Believe that I set up a standard to defend my weakest saints.

All saints can be victorious; trust in me and be steadfast:

I, am your deliverer.

In my glorious Majesty

I work out all your problems in your favor.

Knowledge of me is forever:

Start learning now or whenever:

My work surpasses your full understanding:

Now you see dimly

then, face-to-face it will be clear,

We shall meet on Mount Zion at my appointed time.

Be still, hold your peace, for I am God and God alone."

Supporting Bible References

Matthew 4:10:

"Get thee hence, Satan: for it is written, Thou shalt worship the Lord
thy God, and him only shalt thou serve."

Isaiah 44:6:

"Thus saith the Lord the King of Israel, and his redeemer the Lord of hosts; I am the first, and I am the last; and beside me there is no God."

And God said, "Another Day"

Lord, thank You for another day that You reserve specially for me.
I have done nothing to deserve Your generous favor:
You let me live above my misbehavior
To welcome the buzzing sounds of life all around.

You give me another day to be trained in praising your Holy Name,
Another day to search my soul and see my shortcomings,
Another day to be repentant and seek to do Your will,
Another day to relate to You and bond tightly to You in love,
Another day to see Your blessedness, goodness, and impartiality,
Another day to prepare my heart to meet with You if it's my time to
    depart.

God, You said, "Another day" to learn to be happy in my distress,
And yet coach another to destress.
You give me another day to lift up others in prayer and thanksgiving:
Another day to be with my loved ones of whom I am so fond:
Another day to practice Christian humility and faithfulness to You:
Another day to live for You, fulfilling your purpose for me here.
Abba, Father, thank You for another day, Lord of the day.
I benefit from Your many daily blessings.
Amen.

Supporting Bible Reference

Genesis 8:22:

"While the earth remaineth, seedtime and harvest, and cold and heat shall not cease."

Rescue Us, O Lord:
In A Time Like This

Rescue us, O Lord, rescue us Christians from the cruel and evil
    authorities:
Rescue us, O Lord, rescue us from the darling lions
in a time like this.
Rescue us, O Lord, rescue us from the stealthy black tigers:
They crouch in secret, in
darkness:
They watch, scheme, pursue, and pounce.

Why do they pursue their prey so relentlessly?
They are sore losers from the beginning, and know it. Hoping to win.
They work to humiliate, annoy, distract, afflict to the point of
    suffering and death.
They seek a swift reward, which blinds their senses, understanding,
    and judgment.
They hasten to make their evil desires come to pass.
They try even harder, not willing to give up their plans.
Frustrated, lacking results, but willingly, continuing on, hoping
    to win.
God peeks: He sees; He knows our trials.
He blocks the success of their evil desires:

He says,

"Prove yourselves, my children, for I need you to fit in my perfect
kingdom.

Behold, I AM with you; I protect you,

I shield you:

The black tiger's power to kill you is limited; I cap it:

They can't take your life if I don't let them have it.

Continue in my path; Obey my commands, and praise me.

Don't be afraid or alarmed:

They can't win for I AM with you.

It is I who completely deliver:

I will, in my time. Be patient:

Wait on, my children, wait on,

For the time is drawing near:

In a little while there will be no more tears no more fears:

You who I bless no one can curse:

Hush, be wise; I dry your eyes:

Be prepared:

Study the path of the darling lions and the black tigers,

You will overcome this conflict and many more, too:

Persist in prayer:

Be strong; be vigilant; be faithful:

You will behold your salvation through the power of your God."

Supporting Bible Reference

Jeremiah 1:8:

"'Be not afraid of their faces: for I am with thee to deliver thee,' saith
the Lord."

PART 10

Conclusion

End Time

Time on this present earth will end. God's chosen people will enter eternity with Him.

The soul who finds God finds peace.

Reset Our Lives For God

Signs of end times are being revealed:
Earth feels queer, feels strange in this modern time.
Let your minds dwell upon God's prophecies—
Let your ears hear, let your eyes see!
God's prophecies are being fulfilled.
All of God's words shall come to pass,
Not one jot or tittle shall remain unfulfilled.
Let your minds dwell upon the word of God!
He's a just God, don't slip and fall,
Saints do not belong here,
His redemption of earth is near.

We are God's watchmen and women on the wall.
Saints, give the warning clearly to one and all:
Meditate upon the word of God:
Prepare your hearts, prepare your souls:
Jesus is on His way.
Behold the evils being revealed:
Behold the evil beings unveiled!
Sin's perfection on earth is near
Satan is scared; his time is short:

Reset your lives, reset your hope
Jesus is on His way.

It's time to reset, it's time to reflect
It's time awaken sleeping Laodicea:
It's time to examine and search our hearts:
It's time to put God in His rightful first place.
It's time to be ready to stand for our faith
To stand like a Daniel, like a Paul, like a Stephen,
Like a Mary, like a Pricilla, like a Miriam:
It's time to spend more time with God,
Love God some more; don't excuse Him away,
It's time to reach out,
Be steadfast and sure:
God who made us is grieving for us
Reaching out to us.
It's time to be victorious over appetite, over sin:
It's time to experience Christian victory through Christ.

It's time to put self aside to have no regret.
A time to see God for who He really is.
A time to give Him the glory He deserves and knows.
Power and dominion are His over us:
Time is fleeting, past years don't return:
Time will soon end
This world will be sealed,
Its probation will close forever.
It's time, it's a serious time we are living in.
It's time, it's time, it's time, SAINTS!
It's Time To Reset Our Lives Wholly For God.
Amen.

Going Home

Christians go for a moment's sleep.
They sleep in peace; don't worry; don't weep:
We know that our sleep is precious in the sight of Jesus.
He called, so we had to go:
We all wait at a place where others will follow:
We rest to rise on a distant tomorrow:
All saints will behold their Blessed Redeemer.

We look forward to that great tomorrow
When there will be no more death or sorrow.
I will be waiting for you:

Look out for me too:
We all shall rejoice in going home with Jesus.

Supporting Bible Reference

1 Thessalonians 4:14–17:
"For if we believe that Jesus died and rose again, even so them also
    which sleep in Jesus will God bring with him.
For this we say unto you by the word of the Lord,

that we which are alive and remain unto the coming of the Lord shall not prevent them which are asleep.

For the Lord himself shall descend from heaven with a shout, with the voice of an archangel, and with the trump of God: and the dead in Christ shall rise first: Then we which are alive and remain shall be caught up together with them in the clouds, to meet the Lord in the air; and so shall we ever be with the Lord."

Time Will Stand Still

Time is temporary and can stand still,
It stood still before and will do it again,
Sometime soon, time will end on this earth,
Time will stand still for our eternity to begin.

God will have His will,
His kingdom will come to the earth made new
His will, will be done.
Time will stand still on the earth made new,
Righteousness will flow as a stream as it is in heaven.
Truth will meet righteousness and cleave together:
Time will stand still on the earth made new,
Perfect justice will prevail:
There will be no enemy to attack the redeemed.

Time will stand still when
God will rest from fighting sinfulness:
The earth will delight in its state of sinlessness,
The redeemed shall live in perfect peace,
God's love will overrun the earth made new.
His people will glory and joy in their Savior,

For He will give them life
forever,
What eternal joy that will be when time shall stand still?

Shortly before time stands still:
Jesus will end the sinners' pleas:
The missionary work on earth will end.
The earth will be prepared to unite with its only Creator
When time stands still the earth will be blessed
It will never again experience sinful stress:
We will all enjoy God's sabbath rest,
All the redeemed will lovingly obey and worship God our great
   Creator:
When time stands still
Man will live in peace and harmony with God and his fellow
   creatures:
Man will delight in his new experience after time stands still.
Man's eyes will then see, and his ears hear what God hath prepared
   for him.
All the redeemed shall live in glory for eternity.
Amen

Supporting Bible References

Revelation 10:6:
"And swear by him that liveth forever and ever, who created heaven,
   and the things that therein are, and the earth, and the things that
   therein are, and the sea, and the things which are therein, that
   there should be time no longer."

Isaiah 65:17:

"For, behold, I create new heavens and a new earth: and the former shall not be remembered, nor come into mind."

Isaiah 66:22:

"For as the new heavens and the new earth, which I will make, shall remain before me, saith the Lord, so shall your seed and your name remain."

About the Author

I was born in a Christian family in Jamaica in the West Indies but departed from the faith in my final teen year to practice sinfulness. I realized the spiritual mistake I made in later years, and returned to God with renewed love and understanding of God's principles. I am in again to remain by the power of God. The devil has tried to reclaim me but failed.

My being a part of the Seventh-day Adventist Church at first was my parents' choice, now it's mine from my own conviction, experiencing the love of God.

I am divorced with two adult children and two grandchildren.

I fell in love with Jesus just before my second baptism in October 2003, but more deeply after baptism when more truths about him were revealed to me and my understanding of redemption's story became clear. Previously I was blinded and had a block on the subject, which I could not bear to study. God certainly took care of this.

I grew in love, grace, and favor with God over the years, and developed much spiritual strength and closeness to God. The love of God is far deeper and stronger than mere mortal man can express.

I love Christianity, and with the help of God, practice it as much as is humanly possible. Since baptism, my goal has been to live a sin-free life. I plan to be a Christian until it's my time to depart from this world.

I was called by God shortly after my second baptism to write poems (among other things) about him and to share them with others.

I was inspired at nights or very early in the mornings by holy angels visiting my room, always singing facts about Jesus. At that time, I still had doubts in my mind about Jesus, which I did not share; only God knew my heart. The holy angels grounded my belief in Jesus as the Son of God. The holy angels taught me to write. They came when they thought it was necessary, and repeated messages about Jesus in tuneful lines and verses.

I rejected, not heeding, and they left, only to return seven years afterward. They sang to me repeatedly in my room very early in the mornings. I realized the importance of their visit and started writing.

After I wrote and started sharing with others, the holy angels came no more with messages.

I now write out of abundant love and gratitude to God for selecting me to be inspired by him to write about him. I am not worthy by myself, but by the precious blood of Jesus that covers my transgressions.

I thank God for his special favor to me. I have done nothing to deserve this. Here I have risen to God's desire, his call to service.

I present to you, all Christian saints, this book of religious poems, all about our awesome God. I hope your hearts will be lifted as you let your thoughts soar to heavenly places as you go through the pages. God bless your joyful reading. Amen.